PRAISE FOR SEB DOUBINSKY

"Seb Doubinsky is a great writer, both rambuctious and subtle, who can do anything...Read his work."
        —Jeff VanderMeer, NYT-bestselling author of
        The Southern Reach Trilogy

"Sébastien Doubinsky is among the most important authors writing today, arguably in some realities the most important writer working today."
        —Paul Gallagher, *Dangerous Minds*

"Doubinsky, a self-professed anarchist, is writing prophetic Protest Lit in the classic tradition of Orwell or Huxley."
        —T. E. Grau, author of *The River*

FRAGMENTS OF A
REVOLUTION

ALSO BY SEB DOUBINSKY

THE CITIES-STATES INTERRELATED NOVELS

The Babylonian Trilogy
The Song of Synth
Absinth
White City
Omega Gray
Suan Ming
Missing Signal
The Invisible

POETRY COLLECTIONS

Mothballs
Zen and the Art of Poetry
Spontaneous Combustions
Mountains
This Little Poem

SEB DOUBINSKY

FRAGMENTS OF A REVOLUTION

STALKING HORSE PRESS
SANTA FE, NEW MEXICO

FRAGMENTS OF A REVOLUTION

Copyright © 2021 by Seb Doubinsky
ISBN: 978-1-7340126-4-4

This paperback edition published by Stalking Horse Press, May 2021

www.stalkinghorsepress.com

Design by James Reich
Cover painting: Diego Rivera "Zapatista Landscape" (1915)

Stalking Horse Press
Santa Fe, New Mexico

DEDICATION

To the Subcomandante Marcos, for the accidents of histories, to Paco Ignacio Taibo II, for the domino evenings and to Claudio Bogantes, for the portrait of Zapata hanging on my office wall.

Meditation in the midst of action is a worth a thousand times more than meditation in the midst of peacefulness.

—Hakuin

FRAGMENTS OF A REVOLUTION

« D. C. V. X. V. I. «
—Blaise Cendrars.

PROLOGUE

DARK BIRDS crossed the eye of the sun, burning high overhead like the aura of a vengeful Christ. They weren't vultures yet, but the vultures would come soon enough. The man felt dizzy and the sea replaced the sky.

He tried vainly to hold on to the reins, but slouched slowly to the ground. The horse stopped and waited next to its dismounted rider. The ocean muttered secret prayers. The waves licked the boots of the man lying on the wet sand, arms outstretched, his face turned toward the never-ending blue.

"All this water," he thought, "and nothing to drink…"

His mouth opened with a mute laughter, a web of spit mingled with the salt on his beard. The ocean turned away its powerful shoulders. The horse's ears made a perfect angle.

"If this is death, it is really quiet."

SAN JUAN DEL DESIERTO SONORA APRIL 2ND 1969

1

THE ANGRY MOB stormed the cantina, its double doors slamming open against the stucco walls. The music seeping out of the jukebox was drowned out and the thick cigar smoke was ripped like a theatre curtain. The crowd pushed in front of them a swearing and struggling fat man, his eyes wide with fear. "The eyes of a horse surrounded by flames" Lorenzo thought. Sitting comfortably, he took a sip of his beer, which was as warm and flat as the woman he had slept with last night. He searched briefly for her name, but without luck. The procession trampled by, a few inches away from his boots and—amongst the crowd—he recognized the faces of Marco and Patricio, two of his compañeros on this expedition, energetically twisting the prisoner's arms behind his back. A few women were shrieking hysterically.

"Hang him! Hang him!"

A hand fell on Lorenzo's shoulder and he looked up, startled.

Sven was smiling down at him. "May I sit down?" he asked, pointing at a vacant chair at the Italian's table.

"Sure."

Sven was a young Dane. A month ago, he had been on his way to Mexicali when he had met the small gang in a run-down motel where they had taken refuge for the night. A student in theology at the University of Copenhagen, he had discovered— by chance, in a 1763 Jesuit correspondence—a reference to an old book, El Libro de Esmeralda, which Columbus' astrologist had brought with him to the new world. According to Sven, this book contained very crucial esoteric secrets, linked the school of Odessa, a lost Gnostic society. The last mention of this book dated back to 1867. A French Expeditionary Corp officer, Commander Vinson, himself an amateur of occult studies, had sent a letter to his wife in which he talked about the book a day before getting killed at the battle of Queretaro. According to Vinson, the book could be found in Mexicali. Sven was convinced it was still there. Lorenzo thought his comrade was at least a little crazy, not to say more, but his enthusiasm was contagious, and he had to admit that his quest did add some poetry to this revolution.

"Who's the fat guy?" the Dane asked, waving to the waitress.

"The owner of the general store. All of the village owes him money."

The man fell to his knees, praying in Spanish.

Marco made him stand while a rope travelled from hand to hand through the crowd. A long balcony overlooked the bar. One end of the rope was thrown through its railing, where somebody tied it fast. A noose was made swiftly with the other end. Patricio hoisted the man up onto the counter and Marco, already there, put the noose around his neck.

The grocer suddenly attempted a desperate escape, scrambling with his hands and feet, but to no avail. He found himself with a broken nose and his hands tied painfully behind his back. A moment later, Marco pushed him forward with a strong kick in the ass. The man screamed, gargled, shook, twitched for two long minutes until he finally remained motionless.

Immediately, the bartender poured tequila in an army of empty glasses. To the cheers of the surrounding crowd, a woman emptied her gun into the lump deforming the hanged man's trousers.

"A lot of children look like him," Lorenzo whispered in his neighbor's ear. "That's how some debts were covered…"

Somebody put more coins in the jukebox.

People were laughing.

A group of men began singing revolutionary hymns.

Lorenzo was feeling more and more drunk.

He had woken up early this morning.

He got up to fetch a shot of tequila and Sven followed him like a tranquil bear. The bar was lit up with large beer advertisements. It was still impossible for Lorenzo to put a name on the girl from last night.

"When will we get to Mexicali? the Dane asked, raising the tiny glass to his lips."

"Still thinking about your goddamned book?"

Sven smiled shyly and shrugged.

Lorenzo was about to open his mouth when somebody grabbed his arm.

"Jefe! Jefe! You must come up and see!"

"What? I'm talking to my..."

"Es muy importante..."

Discussion was out of the question. Lorenzo followed the soldier as he pushed some of the other compañeros aside without a word of excuse. Before climbing the stairs to the second floor, Lorenzo turned around to signal Sven he was sorry, and threw his empty glass to him. The Dane caught it in mid-air and held it out to the bartender for a refill.

2

Two HELICOPTERS were circling in the distance.

"Americanos," the soldier said, and spat on the ground.

Standing on the balcony, Lorenzo brought the binoculars up to his eyes. The white star on a blue background crossed the double circle of the bifocals. The U.S. Air Force. That was them, all right.

So far, they had just been observing the situation, and Lorenzo hoped they would stick to observation for a little while longer. The village was some distance from the border and the inhabitants of the region were mostly tuberculosis-ridden alcoholics, who spent most of their time watching soap-operas on television and being exploited by the owners of the hacienda. One shouldn't worry too much. But still, if the Americans already sent observation helicopters in the area, what would they do when the rebels' little troop reached Mexicali?

3

LORENZO RAISED HIS EYES from his book and looked through the window. The Danish countryside was sleeping under its blanket of snow and a few black and twisted trees were tangled together. The coal heater snored at the other end of the room, and he could hear Lena washing the breakfast dishes in the kitchen. Jonas sat on the carpet, drawing with crayons. Mexico was very far away now. He tried to concentrate again on his English edition of Kropotkin's memoirs, but he gave up. Mexico, always Mexico... A few days before, a German anarchist publication had asked him to write an article on his participation in the Rivas brothers' expedition. He hadn't answered them yet.

"What do you think of this, Daddy?"

Lorenzo took up the piece of paper his son was holding in front of him. A plane was bombing houses while people ran in all directions.

"It's very nice...What is it?"

"It's the mean guys bombing the nice guys' camp."

Lorenzo smiled and pressed his son against him.

"That's a horrible story..."

"But you told it to me..." Jonas shrugged and took his drawing back with a pout.

Lorenzo patted the little boy's dark blond hair. Kropotkin fell to the floor and in the kitchen, Lena broke a plate.

4

A FEW HOUSES in the village next to the printer's shop were still burning. Lorenzo screamed that his men should go and take care of the fires, but they were too drunk to react. Lorenzo swore to himself and wondered with anxiety how things were being managed at the hacienda. The owner and his family were being held prisoners there by the revolutionary troops. Sal and Ira, the officers in charge, knew their job well and Lorenzo decided not to worry too much. After all, wasn't the amateurish nature of this insurrection also its nicest aspect? He gave the binoculars back to his subordinate and walked out of the room, going back down to mingle with the happy rumble of the cantina. When he set foot on the last step, the name of the girl suddenly leaped back into his memory.

Soledad.

Of course.

5

PALERMO.

This was long before Mexico, fourteen years ago exactly.

You were seventeen.

You were still holding the gun when the carabinieri arrived. You extended the weapon, butt-first, to the brigadier in charge of your arrest, and you smiled at him. The idiot didn't answer, but told his men to handcuff you. Razelli lay across his bed in his nightgown, half of his brain spilled onto the pillow and sheets. The padrone's room reeked with the smell of powder and blood. The other servants were gathered at the door, watching in silence. As you walked them past, they began to applaud you furiously.

6

THE GROCER was still swinging over the bar. Men drank and laughed, not the slightest bit bothered by the feet grazing their shoulders. Sven was in a heated discussion with two peasants who were trying to convince him of something. The helicopters annoyed Lorenzo. It was the third time this week they had been spotted. He wasn't superstitious but back home three was an unlucky number.

He decided to take a walk in the village to see how things were going. They had secured it during the night, without too much resistance.

Revolution had begun, for good this time, and he was part of it, even though he had absolutely no idea what it might eventually lead to. He heard a clamor and he hurried outside to see. The bulletproof car of the Rivas brothers appeared at the corner of the street, its little black flags flapping happily over big and dusty headlights.

7

"Aren't you coming to bed?"

Lorenzo muttered that he was coming soon and looked at himself again in the bathroom mirror. To say that he had put on a little weight would have been an understatement. He had become fat. In Mexico, he was still slender, and it seemed to him that women found him attractive. Some of them, at least.

"What are you doing, baby? Aren't you coming?" When Lena called him this persistently, it meant she wanted to make love.

He finished brushing his teeth in a hurry. One of his companions had nicknamed him "the Jack of Hearts" back then. That was his precise expression, "the Jack of Hearts."

But was it in Mexico?

8

RICARDO, ENRIQUE, AND THE BROTHER WITH NO NAME (as everybody called him because he never signed the editorials that he published in the anarchist magazines) stepped one by one out of the fat bulletproof car, a 1950 black Cadillac which had belonged to some alcalde. The three raised their arms in sign of victory. The brother with no name and Enrique seemed somewhat tired, but Ricardo was full of energy.

"Comrades!" he began, his little round glasses shining hard under the sun. "Comrades! This day is the first day of the rest our lives—our lives as free men! Comrades, we are proving to Mexico and to the rest of the world that the oppressed can actually free themselves and that a just, classless society is possible on the face of this earth! But today is also only one day among many others and a long road awaits ahead, a road of hopes, fights and victories. To all of you gathered here I say 'thank you' and I urge you to carry on the struggle! The road to justice and freedom is a dangerous one, but we shall overcome! We must not fail. We will not fail! Tierra y libertad, compañeros, tierra y libertad!"

"Tierra y libertad!" The small crowd shouted as one man. A few enthusiasts fired their guns at the sky, and the assembly crowded around the three brothers, who were hugged, one after the other, by peasants, a few women, a lot of soldiers, and even the priest of the hacienda, who had arrived in civilian clothes, escorted by the woman he had always loved.

23

When Lorenzo stepped up in his turn to congratulate the brothers, Enrique winked at him and took him aside. "Come to the hacienda with us. We must talk."

An old woman pushed the young Italian aside and grabbed Enrique Rivas' hand, which she kissed with near religious fervor, leaving a trail of silvery spit on the lawyer's delicate fingers.

9

The hacienda was guarded by soldiers wearing makeshift uniforms, but with determined looks on their faces. Most of them were of Yaqui origin. Twenty bodies were lined up in the yard, covered with a large tarpaulin that some reporters were trying to lift in order to take photographs, in spite of the soldiers' interdiction. Flies buzzed over the scene, provoking a strange ballet of unfinished gestures among the participants.

The brothers Rivas walked ahead, their guns jingling at their side. They were escorted by a group of heavily armed guards. Lorenzo followed them, at a short distance. They had left the bulletproof car at the gate. The brothers' well-polished boots lifted small clouds of yellow dust at each step and it was impossible to tell whether or not they were wearing bulletproof vests under their professorial jackets.

10

WITH SUDDEN DISTASTE, Lorenzo wondered if he actually worshipped the Rivas brothers, as most of the soldiers and the peasants around them did. They had almost arrived at the pink marble staircase of the hacienda, a beautiful 18th Century manor in Spanish colonial style, covered in white and pale blue stuccos. A few bullet holes defaced the walls, like ugly moles. He had to admit that something in the manner which the Rivas brothers spoke, walked, and even laughed, charmed him. Ricardo's eyes, Enrique's hands, the brother with no name's mustache, all were iconic. Lorenzo had rejected icons from the start, though. Revolt, independence, the need for justice, were in some way innate in him. They were the water he drank, the air he breathed, the bullets he fired.

He climbed the flight of steps. Why did it have to be so confusing every time he was trying to think? Lorenzo followed the small party, entering the building. It was much cooler once he stepped inside. The answer to his first question was: in a way, yes.

11

THE MANSION'S HALL was impressive. An immense staircase threatened to crash down like an avalanche of wrought-iron and marble. It was a straight staircase, French style.

In front of him, someone said, "Typically 1860."

He relaxed into the flow, which took him through a labyrinth of Rococo corridors.

Nothing had been touched.

The revolutionaries strolled with nonchalance through the residence, holding tequila bottles and weapons, apparently unimpressed by the surrounding luxury. The Rivas brothers had issued an order forbidding any pillage. All the goods were to be listed and then distributed among the villagers. This hacienda represented three centuries of wealth gathered through the exploitation of the local peasants. What would have been the point, then, in looting something which belonged to you by natural right? It made perfect sense.

Throughout the mansion, a few bloodstains bore witness to the brief resistance they had encountered. In the corridor, a large mirror had been shattered by a bullet. On the ceiling of a boudoir, a little hole resembled a fly. Lorenzo thought about the dead bodies lying under the tarpaulin in the yard. They had died defending a park, a house, a property they would have never been able to afford. He told himself they should write this as their epitaph.

The idea made him smile.

12

UNDER THE COMBINED EFFECTS of wind and speed, clouds can take strange shapes.

It is the same for revolutions.

When the little assembly stopped at last, Lorenzo looked around him, glancing at the small office crowded with cigar-smoking, mustached revolutionaries. He detailed the maps unfolded on the table, the carpet, and the walls, listened to the Spanish exclamations and curses, weighed the guns hanging at the side of his hips, took a deep breath and felt all his muscles relax.

He was home.

13

DOCTOR JENSEN walked into the drawing room, carrying a tray with a bottle of cognac and two glasses. It was four o'clock, time for their afternoon conversation. Lena and Hanna, Doctor Jensen's wife, were still consulting at the clinic for autistic children, while the doctor had finished his work for the day. He put the tray down on the coffee table and Lorenzo folded the newspaper he had been reading. Beethoven's Archduke trio played on the radio. Outside, a small snowstorm darkened the windows. Lorenzo very much enjoyed these daily conversations with his father-in-law. He sometimes wondered even if he hadn't married Lena in order to prolongate them.

"Brrrr, what weather!" the doctor muttered, filling the two glasses quite liberally.

"Will your horses be okay?"

"Oh yes, I have asked Niels to take them to the stables this morning. I can see I was right."

Icelandic horses were the doctor's passion and he owned two of them. Lorenzo liked horses as well, and they often rode together in the countryside, when the weather was good. The doctor leaned toward his son-in-law, and they raised their glass in toast. "Are you alright? You have been looking somewhat preoccupied, these past few days…"

Lorenzo shrugged and smiled briefly. "Yes, yes, I'm okay,

don't worry. It's just that I have an article to write for a German paper and I don't know where to begin…"

"Ah, the infamous blank page…Did you know that even Kierkegaard himself had terrible difficulties writing his texts? He would always postpone them until he couldn't stand it anymore."

Conversation set in. Gradually, the cognac helped Lorenzo forget all about his article. Outside, the wind increased, and the snowflakes began to fly on the horizontal.

14

THE GUARDS were trying to hold back the reporters gathered in front of the office door.

"Cockroaches" Ricardo muttered, nervously playing with his mustache. "Impossible to get rid of them. I wonder who warned them."

Nobody answered.

Anybody with a telephone could have contacted the press, and Ricardo knew this perfectly well. The question was purely rhetorical. "Puta madre." Ricardo seldom swore.

The brother with no name pulled the curtains.

Enrique walked to the dresser, lifting a brandy carafe. "Are there glasses anywhere in this bloody mess?" he asked, turning around to the company.

One of the soldiers offered his plastic cup. "You can use mine. I don't have any diseases. At least, I don't think so."

Everybody laughed and Enrique took the glass.

The smells of weapon grease and powder blended with the cigar smoke. Lorenzo looked at the office walls on which the portraits of the former owners were hanging, perfect gentlemen with Hispanic features. Someone had drawn black mustaches on all of them with a thick marker pen.

15

ALL EIGHT of them were crammed in the little room. Aside from Lorenzo there were Ira, Sal, two soldiers, and the three Rivas brothers. Eight, a magical number. Sven could have told them a lot of things about the significance of the number eight, but he wasn't here. Lorenzo tried to concentrate on the explanations Enrique was giving them, standing behind the desk with a military map of the Sonora region spread out before him.

"I see," Sal said. Sal was an old black man whose scarred face housed a smile made out of gold teeth. He came from Missouri. He had run away at the age of thirteen. He had lived off the lousiest jobs, hoboing from town to town, finally accused of murder in Houston, Texas. He was suspected in the killing of a gas-station manager in a side-street, behind the bar where they had played poker. Sal had lost all of his money to the victim. Ricardo Rivas had been assigned to defend him. Thanks to his tremendous talent, the then-young lawyer had managed to convince the jury of his client's innocence, and Sal had been acquitted. This was a rarity in the state of Texas, where the fate of a black man accused of murdering a white one was usually the electric chair. After the trial, Sal had shared a drink with his lawyer at a local bar, to celebrate.

"I have to tell you the truth" he had said after the second round, leaning a little more over the glasses, "I did kill this man. I wanted his money."

"I know," Ricardo answered, lighting a cigar, "I know very well.

33

And that is exactly why I defended you. You're poor. You live in misery. You see the others exploiting your people and stealing their money. Instead of humiliating yourself again by accepting a lousy job, you chose to become a thief. You understand how this society works and you have reacted logically. Like I always say: Rob the robbers! Excellent."

Sal laughed to the point of tears every time he told this story.

16

THE HEAT was becoming unbearable. Lorenzo could see drops of sweat forming on Enrique's forehead as he talked. The name of Mexicali kept coming back, confirming his intuition: this is their next objective. According to the informants, the city was not very well protected and had the great advantage of housing a weapon depot. The government troops were expecting them to move on Tijuana, attached like every power to the symbolic, the obvious, the conventional. But the rebels would not fall into this easy trap: the name of this revolution was "Surprise."

"Is everything clear, gentlemen?" Enrique asked, looking around the room.

Sitting in a deep leather armchair, Ricardo lit up a new cigar. The brother with no name stood silently against the wall, arms crossed. Sal nodded without a word, looking sombre. Ira scratched his nose and pushed his glasses back against his eyebrows with a nervous finger. One of the Indians, nicknamed Joselito because of his little size, shook his head with approval. The other, an old man named Ignacio whose belly hung over his belt, tightened his jaws and squeezed his rifle. Everybody looked at Lorenzo.

"Perfectly clear, yes," he answered, without knowing what Enrique was referring to, exactly. "Everything is perfectly clear."

17

IT SEEMED LIKE WINTER WOULD NEVER DIE. Sitting at his desk, pushed against a large heater, Lorenzo looked with melancholy at the snow outside, refusing to melt on this sunny March morning. He opened the envelope Hanna had brought him just before leaving for the hospital with Lena. Jonas was at school. Doctor Jensen was in his clinic, taking care of his patients. Silence reigned and Lorenzo was enjoying it. There had been too much noise in his life before. Any regrets? No, no regrets, but too much noise. Thankfully, Jonas had been a very quiet baby. So quiet, as a matter of fact, that for a while they had feared he was deaf, but tests had proven his hearing to be perfectly normal. Lorenzo smiled at the memory of this anguish and shook the envelope over his desk. A postage stamp fell from it, tiny and dark. He took a pair of tweezers and examined it in the light. British Mail, one penny, 1889. It was worth twenty-thousand Danish crowns, at least. Lowering the stamp carefully upon a white china saucer, he picked up the envelope again, and proceeded to decipher the sender's address. London comrades had sent this. He took out a postcard from the drawer and wrote them back, in coded language, that their letter had reached its destination safely. Doctor Jensen came often to look at Lorenzo's stamp collection. He knew nothing about it, but admired Lorenzo's science in the matter when he explained to him why this or that stamp was worth a fortune, because it had been printed upside down, but had been stamped anyway, or because the name of the country had been misspelled. Lorenzo hadn't told him that his 'collection' was a secret bank, a reserve for various anarcho-syndicalist organizations which—when they had money— converted it into stamps that they would send to Lorenzo, to be saved away for hard times. When they needed cash, they would ask him to sell a few. He had conceived of this in Asia, when he had just arrived from Mexico. With the help of a philatelist comrade, stuck like him in Yokohama, they bought old stamps from the Nippon Empire, which they sold back to American collectors. The money enabled them to take a ship to Egypt, where his companion died during a riding trip through the desert, blown to pieces when his horse had galloped over a landmine the English had left behind.

Lorenzo carefully put the stamp away in a thick leather binder. Stamp collector! He let out a deep sigh and closed the heavy volume. What hadn't he done in his life, until now? If only he could remember everything…The clock struck eleven and he sat back at his desk. The letter from the German comrades lay on a corner of the desk, but he chose to ignore it. The sun had come back from behind the clouds. He decided to go for a walk.

18

Gonzalo Diaz y Romero, the owner of the hacienda, lay down his large hand on the shoulder of his wife, who was sitting on a simple wooden chair. Journalists were waiting again outside the door, crammed together with their microphones poised in front of them like Alexander's phalanx.

"No interviews!" Ira repeated, and slammed the door.

Lorenzo sat at the ebony table standing in the middle of the room and pushed a sheet of paper in front of the owner.

"We need your signature." Diaz y Romero looked Lorenzo straight in the eye. He was a tall man, in his forties, his hair drawn back, wearing an Italian suit, and displaying a heavy gold Rolex on his left wrist.

Lorenzo noticed his Adam's apple bobbing up and down behind his pastel pink silk tie. "I guess I don't have a choice." he said, with the voice of one accustomed to giving orders.

His wife took his hand and held it so tightly her knuckles turned white. "Are they going to—?"

Romero gently tapped her fingers and kissed her softly on the head. "Calm down, my dear. I am sure these gentlemen are not barbarians."

Ira chuckled. It was impossible to tell if he meant it as an affirmation, or a threat. He stood against the door, hands in his pockets, his half-opened jacket revealing two 44. caliber revolvers nonchalantly stuck inside his belt.

"So?" Lorenzo asked, becoming impatient. He had always hated melodrama and the couple was beginning to get on his nerves.

"What will you do if I refuse?" Romero asked.

"We'll shoot you, and then we'll ask your wife. If she refuses, we'll shoot her and ask your daughter. And if..."

"Okay, okay!" the man interrupted, wiping his forehead with a white handkerchief. "Give me that paper!"

Lorenzo presented the document to Romero who took it and sat down at the table next to his wife. A fly landed, rubbing its legs on the shiny black flat surface. The owner began to read out loud and impatiently waved the fly away. "I, undersigned, Gonzalo Diaz y Romero, accept to give back the integrality of my fortune and property to their only legitimate owners, that is to say the villagers of San Juan, who have been so mercilessly exploited by my family for five generations. I also hereby renounce to—" He broke off. "The style is terrible, you know that?"

"We don't give a damn. Just sign."

The woman began to cry. She was magnificent, modelled

in a long dark red velvet dress, her hair combed up in a perfect bun. Vaguely, she reminded Lorenzo of a girl he had slept with once, in Paris. She had cried, too.

19

PARIS.

You were nineteen then. Amélie turned her back on you and began to sob. You were feeling wonderfully empty, and you would have rather been alone now, but you held her in your arms anyway. Her blonde hair tickled your nose.

"Was it the first time?" you asked.

She nodded, and you were seized by a strange blending of anger and remorse.

"You should have said so...I would have been more caring..." You felt something wet under your hip and you realized it was a sperm stain, mixed with a little blood. The heat in this chambre de bonne was incredible—or was it your own? You tried to comfort your little Monoprix salesgirl, kissing her tear-covered cheeks, her neck reeking of cheap perfume, her summer-pink shoulders—thousands of tender and hypocritical little kisses to which she had finally succumbed, opening her warm thighs wide for you, but, this time, she didn't cry afterwards.

20

THE DOOR on the other side of the drawing room burst open and a beautiful girl rushed inside. She walked to her sobbing mother and kneeled down to comfort her.

"What have you done to her?" she asked sternly, looking Lorenzo directly in the eye.

Just like her father, he thought.

"For God's sake, what have you done to her?"

Lorenzo felt a cold rage set in. First the wife, now the daughter. This idiot would never sign the paper. They would have to execute him—and with all those stupid journalists hanging around, what awful propaganda that would make! He signalled Ira to take the two women into the other room.

"There you go!" Romero exclaimed, before Ira made his move, pushing the sheet of paper toward Lorenzo.

The revolutionaries looked at him with surprise.

He had signed, after all.

21

"Are you going to execute us, señor?" The woman's voice was strangely calm now.

Lorenzo exchanged a glance with Josélito, who had just walked inside the small room. "No, why?"

The woman shrugged majestically. "People like us are always executed in revolutions."

"Sorry, not in this one."

Her eyes turned to ice.

Lorenzo thought she looked almost disappointed.

Her husband, on the other hand, couldn't believe his ears. "Then what are you going to do with us?" he asked, in a shaky voice.

Josélito stepped in front of his master. He had spent all his life as a stable boy at the hacienda. His voice was soft and clear, without a trace of anger or hatred. "We are going to give you a little house in the village, and we will turn your mansion into a school for the children and a hospital for the villagers. You, señor, will be able to work in the hacienda's gardens. We know you have a passion for flowers. And you, señora, you will be working with the other seamstresses. We know how much you love beautiful clothes. Your daughter, she can teach the children.

She knows how to read and write. If you reject this offer or try to escape, we will execute you. I have spoken."

There was an incredible commotion behind the door. Ira opened it brutally, and half a dozen journalists fell in a heap.

22

LORENZO TURNED OVER on his side and let out a deep sigh underneath the covers.

"What are you thinking about?" Lena asked.

The moon cut out a pale gray rectangle on the ceiling. He sighed again. "It's that goddamned article."

"You don't feel like doing it? Tell them no, it's as simple as that..."

Lorenzo turned over again and put his arm around his wife's shoulder. "It's not that I don't feel like doing it, it's just that I can't remember anything. It all seems so far away. I don't even know if I've ever told you anything about it."

"Oh yes, you have. You did mention Mexico to me, but like the USA, Japan, and Egypt...only in passing. It would be great if you remembered, don't you think? I'm sure you've lived through some incredible things." Lena caressed his fat belly

Lorenzo grunted. "Maybe so, but I can't remember precisely. Everything is so blurred. It's the past, you know? The failed revolutions, the shrunken ideals, the impossible hopes...I've grown old, damn it!"

Lena moved closer, scrutinizing him with care. "Are you regretting?"

"Regretting what?"

"Being here…"

He smiled and kissed her passionately. "No, not all" he said, pulling her to him.

23

LORENZO WAS RESTING in a servant's room under the roof, a sad little room with a sad little chair, a sad little table, a sad little cupboard and a sad little bed, the only furniture. He had given the order that everything in the room should be transported later to the Diaz y Romeros' future house. But for now, he was enjoying the bad mattress on which he was counting to take a well-deserved nap. Ah, the servants' rooms—he knew them so well. It was the best place to doze off and dream about exquisite women.

24

PALERMO.

Some day when you were seventeen, shortly before you shot Razelli. On the bed lay the last edition of Il Libertario, with its pungent smell of cheap paper and fresh ink. The sun cut your miserable room in two halves, golden yellow and dark blue. In a few minutes, you would go back to work at the plantation, but for now you were admiring Patrizia washing herself in front of the white porcelain sink. Her back was long and pale against the shadow-devoured wall. You hadn't fallen in love with her, but with her gestures. She had a certain way of moving her head, of leaning over the pot filled with water, of rubbing her hips. Your temples buzzed. Summer emerged behind your forehead, warming up the inside of your cheeks. You knew Razelli had the hots for her, but you took it as a joke. Desire was your own revolt.

25

SOMEBODY KNOCKED at the door and Ira walked in without waiting for an answer. He looked at Lorenzo lying on the bed. Ira was wringing his hands and seemed very agitated. "I have something to tell you." He sat on the chair.

Lorenzo said nothing, waiting for his friend to go on.

"I am in love," the young Polish Jew said. "I am crazy in love at this very precise moment."

Lorenzo looked at the crucifix hanging on the wall behind his friend's back. It was eaten by worms and Christ had fallen off a long time ago. "So?"

"I have fallen in love with doña Isabela, the daughter of Diaz y Romero. It was beyond me. I looked at her one second too long and that was it. I was supposed to watch over her, but I let her go. She asked me if I could help her escape and I said yes, without hesitation: I have given her some men's clothes, a horse and all the money I had. And do you want to know the truth? I have never been so happy in my life. You can execute me. I am a traitor to our cause."

Ira's eyes had not blinked once. A strange light seemed to radiate from them, but Lorenzo decided it must have been a reflection of the sun which poured through the skylight. He realized he was getting hungry.

"So, are you going to have me executed—yes or no?"

Ira's question interrupted Lorenzo's thoughts. His voice was full of impatience. "You are in a hurry to die, it seems. Why did she want to escape? She didn't want to have to work like all the others? She was too good to teach miserable little Indians covered with skin diseases?"

Ira made an irritated gesture. "She's seventeen. She wants to run away from her parents. She wants to see the world."

A hectic knock on the door interrupted them.

Lorenzo sat up.

The panicked face of a soldier appeared in the open doorway. "Doña Isabela has run away! What should we do?"

Lorenzo looked at Ira, who began picking his nose. "Let her run. She doesn't know what she's missing."

Once the soldier had gone, Ira jumped to his feet and drew one of his revolvers, which he pressed against his temple. "I am crazy about her and I am grateful for what you have just done, but if you don't take care of me, I will!"

Lorenzo smiled, then began to laugh.

Ira looked at him, astounded, and finally put down his gun.

"You know what you are, Ira?" Lorenzo asked him, taking the

gun in his own hand and shoving it back into his friend's belt. "You know what you are? You're not a revolutionary, that's for certain. You're not even a rebel, if you want to know everything. You're a poet, that's what you are. A real poet, like in the old days…Okay, so now cut the crap and get me something to eat, I'm dying of hunger!"

26

As SOON as he set his foot out of the hacienda, after a good meal and a refreshing nap, Lorenzo was assailed by a pack of reporters. They fired questions at him like machine-guns. Flashes crackled. They screamed at him. They pushed him. He almost fell off the flight of steps. After a few minutes of confusion, he stopped in the middle of the courtyard and demanded silence. One by one, the voices became quiet, and soon the only sound was the electric buzz of the tape-recorders. Lorenzo looked around, took a deep breath and began to sing at the top of his lungs:

> *En la plaza de mi pueblo*
> *dijo el jornalero al amo:*
> *"Nuestros hijos nacerán*
> *con el puño levantado."*
>
> *Esta tierra que no es mía*
> *esta tierra que es del amo*
> *la riego con mi sudor*
> *la trabajo con mis manos.*
>
> *Pero dime, compañero*
> *si estas tierras son del amo*
> *por qué nunca lo hemos visto*
> *trabajando en el arado?*
>
> *Con mi arado abro los surcos*
> *con mi arado escribo yo*

páginas sobre la tierra
de misería y de sudor.

Then he added, in the total silence, "Satisfied, gentlemen?"

27

Sven, Marco and Patricio were standing in front of the cantina's counter. The grocer's body had finally been removed and there remained only a little pink bloodstain on the washed floor. A vaguely corrupted smell floated around, but nobody seemed to mind.

"How are things at the castle?" Marco asked, a fresh beer in his hand.

In spite of their names, Hispanicized in solidarity for the Mexican revolutionaries' cause, Marco and Patricio were Frenchmen, former civil servants in the colonies. Sent to the French Indies, they had been so sickened by the inequality there that they started their own revolutionary underground movement. After a tragic strike at the post office, which ended up in the deaths of three postmen and the hospitalization of twenty-fives gendarmes, they fled to Cuba, then to Mexico, where they met the Rivas brothers under mysterious circumstances. Always dressed in black, they were called the Angels of Death and they deserved the name. When oppressors had to get it, they were always the first ones to volunteer.

"Nothing interesting to tell about?" Patricio asked.

Lorenzo shrugged and ordered a beer. Finally, he said, "The little twat ran away."

"What twat?" Sven asked, putting down his glass on the counter. "Romero's wife?"

"No, his daughter."

"You want us to take care of this business?" Marco asked, picking his teeth with a match.

Lorenzo shook his head. "No, it won't be necessary. In a way, it's even good. She'll spread the news. We need this kind of thing. Rumour. It's the most efficient mode of propaganda. Garibaldi himself, as a matter of fact—"

"Speaking of propaganda, did you know there was a radio station very close to Tijuana?" Sven interrupted.

Lorenzo turned to him, very interested. "No, I didn't. Local or national?"

"I don't know, but I would say national. There were too many military police around for it to be regional."

"How did you find the station?"

"It's a pretty strange story, as it happens. I was hitchhiking down to here in order to find my book, and I was picked up by this lunatic. A dentist travelling from town to town. He even asked to check my teeth before I got in his car. The back seat was crammed with a clown costume and props he used to relax his patients—at least, that's what he said they were for. Anyway, to cut a long story short, we got lost one night near Tijuana. We drove around until, finally, we saw some lights in the distance. We thought it could be a motel. Big mistake. It was a television station, like I told you before. It was swarming with MPs and that idiot and his jokes almost had us shot."

Lorenzo thought for a second. "Could you find this place again?"

"I think so. But like I said, it's heavily guarded and those guys mean business."

They heard shouts behind them. Two journalists were arguing across a table where a woman sat, her face hidden by the shadow. The journalists each grabbed the other's throat and rolled together on the floor, screaming like hogs. The woman leaned forward to rescue her glass of wine. As her face moved into the light, Lorenzo recognized Soledad. She winked at him with a mysterious smile. He winked back and turned around to order another beer, his heart incredibly light and joyous now, after the long day he just had.

28

IN THE VILLAGE, evening had fallen and so had the temperature. Lorenzo walked alone in the deserted streets, shivering once in a while because of the chilling breeze that came up from the desert. He felt drunk and happy. Tomorrow they would head for Mexicali. Their first real city. A flash of expectation and anguish ran down his spine.

A thin silhouette appeared at the corner. Soledad. She seemed drunk too. His life had been full of women like her. Strange stories, distant stars. He stopped and lit a cigarette, remembering names of exotic brands of tobaccos. She sat by his side.

"I missed you" she said. She smiled and her teeth seemed very white in the darkness.

He took her by the arm, and they strolled up the main street, raising a slow ochre cloud behind them, whispering sweet words and promises in each other's ear—the crazy magical promises every revolution brings.

MEXICALI
APRIL 5TH 1969

1

LORENZO STOPPED to admire the pair of guns shining in the shop window. He loved guns so much he sometimes wondered if he hadn't become a revolutionary just because of them. Nothing was more surprising than to fire a shot: the adrenalin flash, the jumping of the wrist and the heat in the shoulder, the smell of cordite and, finally, at the end of the buzzing…Death…He would never forget the satisfaction he felt when he killed for the first time. Razelli's corpse seemed sublime. He had grown out of it since, but the image remained.

The streets were packed with people. If not for the black flags hanging from the balconies, he thought, one would have never believed a revolution had occurred here just a few days ago. It seemed like the whole city was participating in a joyous funeral. He looked at the reflection of the flags in the shop window. They made his eyes seem even darker.

The revolvers were English, with ebony pistol grips. He wondered how much these little beauties could be worth, and why nobody had taken them. Money had been abolished on the very evening the city was conquered, and bartering was declared the sole commercial exchange system. Yes, those guns must have been worth a fortune. Too expensive for the people living here anyway. After all, Mexicali wasn't exactly on the wealthy side, apart for its weapon depot. He scratched his neck. He really needed some new guns. His old automatics couldn't shoot straight anymore and had already jammed twice.

A truck drove down the main street, a band playing full blast on its platform. Three teenagers with electric guitars and a tiny drum set stuck between empty fruit crates. Three young girls—their girlfriends, no doubt—sat at their feet, laughing and drinking beers. The drummer was terrible. A few newspaper sheets whirled in the trail of the vehicle and the music diminished until it became a simple buzzing which was soon swallowed by the rest of the city noises.

A TV crew appeared on the opposite sidewalk and began to interview passers-by. Lorenzo couldn't identify either the reporter's accent or the little flag stickers on the cameras.

But those guns…

Lorenzo folded his arms across his chest. The sun was getting really hot now and his t-shirt stuck to his back. His skull was beginning to overheat too, in spite of the black Stetson he wore. He had found the hat during the assault on the city. He scratched his chin and looked at a big sign hanging over the street, a few hundred meters from where he was standing. It displayed a half-naked woman with generous curves. The building was the brothel where he had found a room on the first night. Prostitution had been abolished and all the pimps executed, but as most of the girls didn't know any other work, the revolutionary committee had decided to keep the place open and tolerate the activity, as long as no money was used in the transactions. You could barter a lot of things against a little loving.

A drop of sweat rolled into his eye. Two women passed behind him, chatting in Spanish. He loved this language, so close and yet so far from his own. He turned around to take a look at them. They were just fat ladies going to the market, their bags filled with fruits. He turned back to the guns in the window.

A decision had to be made.

He pushed the glass door open and stepped inside to the sound of a joyful chime. A little old lady looked suspiciously at him from behind her counter. She was in her late seventies—at least. Her face was so wrinkled that her eyes looked artificial. They pierced through the wrinkles with a shiny, magical glow, almost beautiful in the middle of all her painted mummified flesh. Her hair was pulled up in a tight bun and dyed the color of dried blood. Lorenzo flashed a smile.

She didn't smile back. "What do you want?" the creature croaked.

He realized one of her eyes was made of glass. It didn't move, while the other rolled crazily from one side to the other. "I am interested by a pair of guns you have in your window."

The old woman raised her chin toward the front of her shop. "The ones with the ebony grips?"

Lorenzo nodded.

"What can you offer me for them?"

He walked to the counter and leaned over her. "A kiss."

The woman raised her good eye in surprise. "A what?"

Lorenzo seized the ruined face between his palms and pressed his lips against her reddish mouth, harder and harder. Searching between the toothless gums, he finally encountered a small animal, surprisingly gluttonous and active. He felt the shoulders of the woman tighten, then relax. Two hands joined behind his neck.

"Take them" she said.

When he walked out of the shop, she told him he could come back whenever he wanted and winked at him with her good eye. Well, he thought it was with her good eye.

2

A TRAVELLING THEATRE had set up at the corner of the street, using a black and red flag as background curtain. Lorenzo was getting tired of this cheesy color symbolism. His own t-shirt was dark blue, his pants were black and his boxer-shorts pale blue. So there.

The actors played a conventional farce, with the bad capitalists and the good revolutionaries. Lorenzo watched them for a while, until he was distracted by a much more pleasant scene: a pair of magnificent black eyes staring at him from the other side of the crowd.

"Patrizia!" he muttered, taken by emotion.

Of course, it wasn't her.

3

PALERMO.

Patrizia turns her beautiful black glance toward you and you laugh. You swim closer to her in the little creek, seaweed on your head like a stinking wig. She sits on the rocks, the bottom of her long black dress soaked in the salty spume. "Beware of the fishermen, they might mistake you for a shark!" she giggles, splashing salted water in your face with both her feet.

You were born on the same day and you just turned fifteen.

Soon you are going to kiss for the first time.

4

It wasn't Patrizia. Still, one never knew. Things could be strange, these days. The young woman was dressed in a short yellow dress, showing a lot of cleavage. Lorenzo felt his heart beat faster and held the package wrapping his new guns closer to his chest.

"Die, you banker swine!" the Revolutionary commanded on the stage and his mustache fell from his face, raising laughs from the crowd.

"My money! My money!"

The woman hadn't moved. Lorenzo came closer. She was looking at him as if she knew him. His step became less assured and he felt his mouth dry up. It had been years since he had walked like this toward a woman.

5

LENA WAS ASLEEP, lying on her side. He let his hand run along her beautiful back in the darkness. His wife. The mother of his child. When he had met her for the first time in Paris, upon his arrival from Egypt, he would have never thought he would use such words, someday. He would remember this 14th of July ball for the rest of his life—the crowd, the firecrackers and the thousands of little blue-white-red flags everywhere. He had lost the friends he had arrived with and sat, completely drunk, on the steps of the Saint-Etienne-du-Mont church. A young woman with dishevelled blonde hair sat down next to him and began to cry. She had just seen her boyfriend kissing another girl in front of the Panthéon. Lorenzo offered her some wine from his bottle and they quickly fell in love. They saw each other again and began to construct their story: the apartment on the Rue de la Clé, Jonas, their move to Denmark so that she could finish her psychology studies and, today, this quiet and comfortable life sharing her parents' house, in Møldrup, near Vejle, this life he would have never imagined possible. If somebody had told him that in Mexico... Some images flickered in his mind, but they were mostly of flames and a little coal. He seemed to have no regrets about that expedition and yet he could remember nothing with precision. Lena called this "a mental block." It might be true. When, at times, he had mentioned his adventures, he had always exaggerated the exotic and the anecdotal, and it felt to him like he was inventing more than relating. Lena laughed in her sleep. He kissed her cheek and lay his head back on the pillow. The wind was blowing in the cold night. He hoped it would blow away the conflicting feelings that clashed in his soul, but he knew that was impossible: the wind only cares about the wind.

6

A LOUD MOTORCYCLE with a sidecar drove by, very close to them. The young woman was startled and grabbed Lorenzo's arm, then she blushed. They resumed their walk under the shadowy arcades. Her name was Teresa. She wasn't born on the same day as him. She was two years younger. She was beautiful nonetheless and worked at the only cinema in town.

"When I saw you earlier, I really thought I knew you" she said, shyly. "It sounds kind of stupid, doesn't it?"

Lorenzo shook his head. "No, not at all, I had the same feeling."

Teresa grasped his arm a little tighter. "Was she beautiful?"

"Who?"

"The woman I made you think of."

Lorenzo avoided a kid dressed in a mourning costume running toward him. "Yes, very." The silence mingled with the white light, cutting the street in two. "And the man I reminded you of?"

"Yes, he was very handsome too."

"Was?"

She turned her face and didn't answer. Lorenzo felt like

another face was imperceptibly covering his own, but he told himself that it was only an effect from the breeze blowing between the arcades.

7

THEY ARRIVED at the town square, framed by baroque buildings and Guadalupe palm trees bent by the heat. A multitude of smells from spices, fruits, animals and pastries whirled in the air from the market. Lorenzo saw with satisfaction that bartering worked out fine. The Rivas' bulletproof automobile was parked in front of City Hall, which they had turned into their headquarters. Soldiers came and went between the stands, their weapons casually hanging from their shoulders. Someone called Lorenzo's name and he noticed Sal and Marco waving at him from a café terrace. Two other guys were with them, but Lorenzo didn't know who they were. "Let me introduce to you Teresa" he said, taking a seat.

"Pleased to meet you," Sal answered, rising politely. "This is Joe and Manuel. Joe is an American. Manuel is Spanish. They just enlisted in our brigade. Joe has a motorbike. It can be useful. Manuel is an artist. This can be useful too. Well, that's what the brothers believe, at least."

They laughed and Marco ordered another round.

A bird landed on a branch and began to sing. An orchestra attacked a popular tune in a storm of wrong keys. Teresa slipped her foot over Lorenzo's. A chubby waitress brought the glasses. Lorenzo took his cigarettes out. Life was a whirlwind of memories and surprises. He looked at Teresa, who discreetly winked at him.

"Has anybody seen Sven?" Marco asked.

8

LORENZO BRUTALLY AWOKE from his dream and sprang up in his bed. Evening had set in and the room was dark. The space next to him was empty, but Teresa's perfume still floated around him. He turned on the light and blinked a couple of times. It felt like he had dreamt about the day that had just passed, but he wasn't sure. The gates of his dream slowly closed, and he realized he was hungry.

Screams and laughter exploded from the corridor while he was getting dressed. He recognized Sal's voice, joking with one of the girls. Lorenzo grabbed his belt. His new guns shined in the light. He couldn't wait to try them.

9

THE SITTING ROOM at the bottom of the stairs was bathed in a soft reddish light. An old jukebox spilled out vintage romances. A large antique clock indicated it was eight thirty in the evening. He had gone up to his room with Teresa around five—he remembered one of the girls making a bad joke about "tea-time."

A few customers chatted with the girls on the round sofa in the middle of the room, others were putting their jackets back on, familiar scenes from before the revolution. Lorenzo had thoroughly discussed the subject with the Rivas brothers, once. Could they, as anarchists, tolerate prostitution as a legal means to earn a living? Ricardo had shrugged and admitted that he had no opinion on the subject. Enrique had coughed, embarrassed, and then argued about principles and reality. The brother with no name was the only one who had actually said anything, really, mentioning the fact that the pirate communities in Tortuga in the 17th century were founded on a communist basis, but used slave labor. Everybody had shaken their heads in the most intelligent manner, without really understanding the analogy, as was so often the case when the brother with no name's spoke. They had spent the rest of the evening smoking and playing cards, without mentioning the subject again.

Lorenzo took out his cigarettes and looked around. Teresa was gone all right. Sven was discussing something with an old Gypsy woman at a table. On the couch, a soldier with a dishevelled uniform leaned over the chest of a fat blonde girl and nibbled at a tit springing out of her bodice. Lorenzo moved closer to the table where the Dane had his cards read.

The Gypsy woman put a card down on the table. "The Chariot. You are lucky, young man, the Chariot, that's sure success. However…"

"However?" Sven looked worried.

The old lady drew another card, which she put on top of the first one, nodding to herself. "That's what I feared. The Wheel of Fortune. Your quest isn't over yet, my boy. You have to move on. To Tijuana, for example. There is nothing for you here."

Sven let out a deep sigh, discouraged.

Lorenzo lay down a hand on his friend's shoulder.

10

SVEN AND LORENZO walked down the main street in silence. The motorcycle with the sidecar slowed down to match their speed and followed them along the sidewalk. "Can I give you a lift somewhere?" Joe asked. He was the American who had enlisted that morning.

"We're going to the restaurant on Plaza Mayor."

"Come on, hop in!"

Sven sat in the sidecar while Lorenzo clung to Joe's back. They left in a sound of rattling thunder and the laughter of kids playing war.

The bike's vibrations lulled Lorenzo. The city was filled with sounds and colors mixing with the dusk. Fireworks exploded. Radios were blasting. Bursts of laughter—real laughs for once, happy laughs—sounded like trumpets. Strangers greeted one another, shook hands, exchanged news. The revolution seemed to have awakened a long-forgotten humanity, and it might have very well been the first revolution to manage that.

11

PALERMO.

You must be about six years old.

The fire burns and growls in the fireplace. You are sitting on your mother's knees, your cheek buried in her bosom. She comes from the North. That is why you are called Lorenzo, like Il Magnifico. It's evening. The old women talk while their husbands suck on their cheap pipes. Most of the children are already in bed. You are the oldest, so you can stay up a little longer. So can Patrizia. She's sitting with her aunt, in the corner. Her mother died last year, and her father is in America. Every Christmas, her father sends her a letter, in which he tells he will be back soon. He has been away for five years now. Old Martha, the village's midwife, tells the story of a revolutionary ghost who helped Garibaldi in the region. In the harsh tobacco smoke, everybody is listening. A log explodes in the fireplace, sending tiny sparks all around, toward emptiness, toward darkness, toward nothing.

12

LORENZO WAS SORTING the stamps from a new package when Jonas walked in, a sheet of paper in his hand. Lena was resting on the leather sofa, watching a program on autistic children, her research field. Lorenzo raised his head and frowned. "You're still not in bed? It's after nine o'clock."

Jonas ignored his father's remarks and put the paper right under his nose.

"Watch out for the stamps. Come here—there you go!" he said, taking his son on his lap. "What have we here?"

Jonas shrugged. He had a smile of shyness and pride. "The teacher asked us to write a story on our favorite animal, so I wrote this. Here, read it."

Lorenzo approached the board-lamp and began to read out loud.

"No, not like that," his son protested. "Read it secretly."

Caressing his son's blond hair, Lorenzo concentrated again.

The Storie of the bare.

Once uppon a time there was a bare who lived in a big forrest. He was the King of the Bares and he had the loudest voice. When he shouted, all the men hidd and shook like leves. One day, a little boy was walking alone in the forrest and he got lost. He couldn't find his way back and he began to wheep. He was a very nice little boy, who was called Emanuel. He whept and whept and finaly he fell asleep under a tree. The king of the bares found him and said to himself:

"This little boy is very cute. I will eat him."

He opened his mouth, like this, to eat him, but Emanuel woke up and shouted: "Don't eat me! I am Emanuel, a nice little boy and my father is the King of the Unters. If you save my life, he will give you a prezent."

The King of the Bares thought about this for a seccond and said: "Ok, climb on my back, I will take you home. But I do hope your father will give me a prezent."

So the bare took Emanuel home as he had promissed. But when Emanuel's daddy saw the bare, he killed him imediately with a bullet and stripped his skin. Emanuel began to cry at first, but he was glad afterwards because his daddy had made him a covver with the bare's skin and it was very warm in the winter.

Lorenzo shook his head and stroked his beard.

"So," Jonas asked him, his eyes shiny with hope, "what do you think of it?"

Lorenzo smiled and put the paper down on the table. "You showed this to your teacher yet?"

The boy shook his head. "No, I just wrote it."

Lena got up from the sofa and picked up her son. "Enough chat for now, Mr. Writer. Time to go to bed."

Lorenzo kissed his son and winked at him. "Tell me what your teacher says, ok?"

13

Joe parked in front of the restaurant. Lorenzo and Sven got off the motorcycle as the American cut off the engine. The Rivas brothers were sitting on the terrace with their officers. Old Martha had never talked about a revolutionary ghost. Lorenzo was puzzled. The memory had been so clear, so real. He shook the three brothers' hands and joined their table. Manuel, the artist, took out some sketches for propaganda posters. Drinks were served. The drawings moved from hand to hand. Lorenzo thought they were excellent. They ate. They laughed.

A band gathered around the table and sang a recently composed hymn to the Rivas brothers. Ricardo stood up and thanked them profusely. One of the musicians—the oldest of the group—had tears in his eyes. Sven arrived in his turn and sat next to Lorenzo. Enrique proposed a toast to the inhabitants of Mexicali. They applauded together and raised their glasses. Lanterns were lit over the tables and the first mosquitoes of the evening arrived, interrupting the conversations from time to time as the revolutionaries slapped at their own faces.

14

AFTER DINNER, all the officers joined the Rivas brothers in the drawing room of the restaurant to discuss strategy. French cognac and Cuban cigars. Lorenzo brought up the question of the television station. It might be smart to take it before marching on Tijuana: they could shower the region with propaganda prior to the offensive. Enrique and the brother with no name listened to him closely, but Ricardo disagreed. They hadn't enough men yet, to risk losing some in a very hazardous expedition. True enough, a lot of men had joined their ranks, but they still needed a lot of training.

Sal agreed. He was the man in charge. "They're really enthusiastic, that's for sure, but good God, what a bunch of fucking goofballs!"

Sven interjected: "We cannot wait for two weeks! The government troops are going to counterattack soon, and Mexicali is impossible to defend. We have to move on to Tijuana and build our defenses there. It's essential: with Tijuana in our hands, other regions might join us. We have contacts with Chiapas, Oaxaca, Chihuahua and even some students from Mexico City have sent us messages of support. They're just waiting to start their own uprisings. The trade unions are preparing for major strikes. No, we cannot wait!"

Lorenzo wondered if Sven was sincere or if he only thought about his goddamned book. But he had to admit that what the Dane had said made sense.

They talked for a few hours more and finally voted by a show of hands to march on Tijuana exactly a week from that day. Sal promised his new troops would be ready by then. Joe and Lorenzo would go on a recon mission a few days before. They would resolve the question of the television station later. Entertainment could wait.

15

LORENZO FOUND himself standing at the bar next to the American, half-empty glasses in front of them. They were the only ones left in the restaurant, with the exception of Manuel, who was sleeping, mouth wide open, in an armchair in the lobby. The bartender had gone to bed and had left them the keys of the place. At this hour, revolution needed fuel.

"Where are you from?" Lorenzo asked.

"New York."

"Beautiful city."

"Some say so. You ever been there?"

"I lived there for a few months."

Joe's leather jacket shined under the bar's lights. There was something written in the back, but it was half erased.

"You've got a great jacket" Lorenzo said, "but aren't you too warm?"

The American smiled.

"I'm dying of heat."

"Why aren't you taking it off, then?"

Joe shrugged and finished off his glass.

"It's a long story. This jacket is actually not mine. It belonged to a very close friend. His name was Kurt. We belonged to the same motorcycle club in New York. He got shot one night by the cops. It was a mistake, they were looking for someone from a different gang, but they couldn't tell the colors in the dark. He should have been buried in this jacket, but his family wouldn't have it. They dressed him up in a ridiculous three-piece suit and I kept this jacket. I never take it off, except when I sleep or when I fuck—and even then, not every time."

Lorenzo decided it was time to stop asking stupid questions. Silence fell again, interrupted occasionally by Manuel's snores, his arms crossed over his sketch book.

16

THE BROTHEL where Lorenzo lived was open twenty-four hours a day. A sign in the window, handwritten in large red letters, read: Live animals are not accepted as payment anymore. "The joys of bartering" Lorenzo thought, walking in. In the drawing room, Marco and Patricio were playing cards.

Lorenzo sat at their table and lit a cigarette. "What are you playing?"

"French tarot" Marco explained, turning over a card.

"I thought tarot cards were used to tell the future."

"Not in France. There is no future there."

Patricio laughed and picked up the hand.

"Can I play with you? Will you teach me?"

"No. It would take too long and you are too drunk."

"You're absolutely right."

Lorenzo took a long drag and watched the two Frenchmen. After a little while, he felt his head sink over his chest. It was too late to react. He fell into a deep sleep.

17

SKELETONS ON HORSEBACK galloped through the streets, shooting their guns in the air while escorting the brothers Rivas' car, also driven by a skeleton. Marco and Patricio sat at a café terrace, playing cards, but they were only drawing spades. Old Martha walked around, leaning on her cane, but she was just a ghost. A young woman who looked like Patrizia took his hand and asked him, "Where is your mommy?" He couldn't remember in which pocket he had put her. The woman suddenly let out a scream. He woke up in a start.

18

"I'm so sorry, I didn't want to scream like that." Teresa stood in front of him, her hand still covering her mouth.

"I dropped by to see you. I know it is late, but I just got off work. The last movie begins at twelve and it's a pretty long feature. I didn't notice you in the dark. I thought you were dead."

Two girls peeked over the top of the staircase, looking worried, but Lorenzo explained the situation and the girls disappeared, muttering insults.

THE LIGHT of the neon sign blinked across the floor with surprising regularity, given the state of the local electricity. Lorenzo had his arm around Teresa's shoulders and was smoking a cigarette. The blue smoke rose to the ceiling, where it disappeared into the shadow.

"When you told me that I reminded you of someone this afternoon, who were you thinking about, exactly?" Teresa's voice was soft and tranquil.

Lorenzo sighed and shook his head. He didn't feel like answering.

"An early love, I guess... All men have an old flame which eats at them and prevents them from falling in love again. At least, that's what they say, every time." She took the cigarette from his lips and inhaled.

Lorenzo laughed in the darkness and smoke. "Yes, you're right. Her name was Patrizia. She was my fiancée in Italy. We were working together in an olive tree plantation, near Palermo. We were engaged. We were promised to each other since we were fifteen and that was okay by us. One day, Razelli, the owner, kidnapped her and raped her. I killed him. I was arrested, I ran away and here I am."

"Such a romantic!" She turned around and grabbed the

tequila bottle from the side table. She took a sip, wiped her mouth and offered it to Lorenzo.

Grabbing the bottle, he realized he couldn't see her beautiful black eyes in this darkness and thought it was really a shame.

SOMEWHERE ON THE ROAD BACK FROM TIJUANA APRIL 12TH

1

THE MOTORCYCLE made a hellish noise on the rough trail. In the sidecar, Lorenzo was getting so shaken up he felt as if his eyes were bouncing against each other. He held on tightly to the camera with the massive zoom lens that he had used to take pictures of the enemy defenses. A bag filled with shot film lay between his feet. In his thick pilot goggles, Joe looked like a giant insect. They desperately needed gas.

Two hours ago, the reserve jerrycan had fallen to the ground when the jeep hit a pothole, and it had exploded against a stone. They couldn't afford to run out of gasoline in these parts: the region was controlled by regular troops and they had already, by some miracle, avoided two patrols. Suddenly, Joe yelled and pointed to the horizon.

Lorenzo thought he saw a vague shape. A gas station. In the middle of this desert? He clenched his jaws to prevent his teeth from shattering. After all, why not? He had seen stranger things since arriving in this goddamned country. The gas station was probably abandoned anyway. He crossed his fingers, nonetheless.

2

DOCTOR JENSEN trotted ahead on the muddy trail. They had taken advantage of a precarious improvement in the weather to go for a ride. For his last birthday, Lorenzo's father-in-law had given him a horse, a sturdy grey Icelander. Lorenzo had immediately taken to the horse because he thought it resembled him: the animal had a fat stomach which rolled along when he trotted, and he would never do what his rider commanded. It was called Fafnir. The doctor went into a gallop to loosen his horse's legs. Lorenzo watched him diminish in the distance and thought about an episode in Mexico when the horse of one of his companions had panicked and galloped straight into a minefield. He tried to remember the name of the man and he realized the scene had taken place in Egypt. The guy's name was Josh, he was an Englishman. Lorenzo pressed the flanks of his horse and set to catch up with his father-in-law, who had disappeared into the woods. When Lorenzo met up with him, the doctor had dismounted and was clearing a large stone covered with dried grass.

"Come have a look…"

Lorenzo got off his horse. The stone was now perfectly visible, and he saw engraved markings on its surface.

"These are runes," the doctor explained. "This was an old Viking ceremonial place. I found it by chance, a few years ago, stopping to let Hriminir rest." The horse puffed at the mention of his name and stepped closer to his master, who caressed his nose.

Lorenzo took a closer look at the markings. "What do they say?"

The doctor cut a little branch with his Swiss-Army Knife. "I asked a friend of mine, who is an archaeologist, to translate them for me. He wasn't able to. They're too damaged. The only name he could read was Bragi, the god of poetry."

"And of memory, too, if I'm not mistaken?" Lorenzo added, happy to contribute. "I think I read about this somewhere."

Doctor Jensen shrugged and began to sharpen the branch. "The Vikings didn't have a god for memory. Actually, I don't think any civilization ever had. The Greeks had a muse, Mnemosyne. A muse, not a Goddess. Maybe it was a form of compensation. Memory belongs to men, I suppose."

Loreno muttered, "Yes...and that's where all the problems come from."

3

THE GAS STATION wasn't abandoned, as Lorenzo had initially feared, but it wasn't exactly a model of efficiency. The pump attendant was a nearly blind old man, rocking in a chair in front of his office. Joe filled up the motorcycle's tank and Lorenzo extracted himself from the sidecar to exercise his legs. His thighs were stiff, and his knees were wobbly. The tank full, Joe gave the old man a handful of keyrings, decorated with a black flag motif, as payment. The brother with no name had this idea to facilitate trade. There also were pens with the portraits of Proudhon, Bakunin and Kropotkin, pocketknives and matchboxes illustrated with revolutionary scenes. These items were much more useful than money.

The old man weighed the keyrings suspiciously in his hand. "Now what the hell are these?"

Joe explained.

The old man shook his head. "Revolution, eh? What do you know about revolution?"

"And you?" Lorenzo replied defensively. He had always despised old farts, but the man didn't seem to care. He let out a little laugh.

"Oh me, I was with Zapata, so..."

Lorenzo put his hand against the doorframe. "With Zapata?"

The old man giggled again, rocking faster in his chair. "I was seventeen. I was young. What a blast we had."

4

THEY STOPPED a few hours later to rest and have some lunch in the shadow of a large rock. The sun was sailing toward afternoon. What struck Lorenzo the most, now that they were resting, was the silence. He had never heard anything like it, apart from the moment after he had shot Razelli.

Joe took out the food from his backpack and sat down in front of him. They ate and drank without exchanging a word. Joe wasn't the talkative kind. Lorenzo offered him a cigarette, which the American accepted. A match caught fire in the heat. Their mission had gone well. They had obtained all the information they needed. Joe lied down on the ground, his neck resting on a fat stone. A black insect zoomed over them. Lorenzo let out a blue plume. "What do you think about all this?" he finally asked Joe, who was enjoying his smoke, eyes closed. The silence was getting on his nerves.

"About what? The revolution?"

"Yes, all that stuff."

Joe shifted to a more comfortable position. "We're having fun, aren't we?"

Lorenzo smiled and shook his head. "Yeah, you're right. We're having fun."

Silence fell again, but Lorenzo didn't find it as heavy as before.

MEXICALI
SAME EVENING
APRIL 12TH

1

WHEN THE FILMS WERE SENT TO THE LAB, Enrique Rivas insisted on congratulating Joe and Lorenzo personally. "I don't know what this revolution would be without guys like you," he said with a smile that made both ends of his moustache touch his cheeks.

"I don't either," Lorenzo answered, only half-joking.

2

JOE AND LORENZO were exhausted and decided to have a cold beer. When they walked into their regular bar, a small rathole right across from the cathedral, they were surprised to find the place crowded. About fifty young people with pink and happy faces were screaming at the top of their lungs over the juke-box melodies. Joe and Lorenzo stood at the bar. All the tables were taken. "What's going on?" they asked the bartender, whom they knew well.

He leaned toward them with a look of disgust. "Students. They come from California and Texas—by bus..."

Lorenzo peeked over his shoulder and drank a sip of his cold beer. "What the fuck are they doing here?"

The bartender shrugged. "They heard it was party time every day here. So, they decided to crash the party!"

Lorenzo was curious. "What do you make them pay with?" The revolution had abolished money.

"With their dollars, what else? You think I'm stupid or something? If it turns bad down here, I'm going to go bother them at their home!"

A pretty blonde with vague eyes called the bartender, who excused himself. Joe and Lorenzo finished their beers in silence. There was nothing funny in the laughter they heard behind them.

3

THE NIGHT was at its darkest now, but the party rolled on. Drunk tourists stumbled out of the bars and sang beneath the lanterns. Firecrackers exploded sporadically. Three large American buses with air-conditioning were parked behind the cathedral. A group of alcohol-soaked students was screaming at the corner of the street.

"Viva la Revolucíon! Amigos! Amigos!"

They waved their cheap bottles of tequila in the air while their girlfriends giggled like hens.

All of this was incredibly sad.

Joe hadn't once broken his familiar silence. On the way back to their pension, his long silhouette was like a ghost under feeble lights of the lanterns.

TIJUANA
APRIL 18TH

1

IRA GROANED on his stretcher. A bullet had smashed his shoulder and his right leg was broken in three places from the fall. Without morphine, the pain was unbearable. About fifty men lay wounded around him, some on stretchers, others on the bare ground. The Alcazar, the largest cinema in town, had been turned into a field hospital, the local clinic having burned down during the first hours of the attack. Lorenzo clutched the hand of his companion.

Ira briefly opened his eyes. Sweat had gathered over his eyebrows. "My…glasses…?" he managed to say.

Lorenzo looked inside the pocket of his jacket and took them out. "There you go. They're intact. You're one lucky bastard! You fell from some height, you know that?"

Ira had posted himself on the second-floor balcony of the central police station. He fell over the railing when the bullet hit him. He smiled through the pain and clenched his jaws. "And…what about…my leg?"

"The doctor said you'll be able to walk again. You'll limp like a duck, but you'll walk." Lorenzo felt a presence beside him and turned to see who it was.

Manuel, along with Sven and a very pretty young woman wearing men's clothes, who looked vaguely familiar. "How is he?" the Spaniard enquired.

"He's ok. Well, it could be worse."

The girl stepped forward and looked down at the wounded man. Lorenzo could feel a great tenderness in her eyes. "She insisted in coming to see him" Sven explained. "As she fought on our side, I said all right. You don't very often meet a woman who can shoot as well as she does. I only met one before, in Aalborg. She used to go hunting with her father. She killed him during a boar hunt. They could never find out if it was an accident. The old man was a real tyrant. Nobody cried at his funeral, not even his wife. Right between the eyes. I was supposed to marry her, but after that I hesitated and finally chickened out. You've only got one life, right?"

The girl was now kneeling next to Ira. She wiped his forehead with a handkerchief. The wounded man opened his eyes again.

He looked surprised. "You?"
She smiled and this smile was so gentle that the three healthy revolutionaries coughed at the same time, embarrassed. "Yes. I have never forgotten what you have done for me."

It struck Lorenzo like lightning. Doña Isabela! Diaz y Romero's daughter, that this idiot had helped escape! This revolution was really getting out of hand.

2

LORENZO PATROLLED a small street in the town center, followed by seven of his men, progressing with their guns pointed toward the windows. Recon mission. Most of the strategic objectives had been taken after the first two days of the assault, but the central fort was still resisting and there were snipers everywhere. Joe zoomed by on his motorcycle, a clutch of hand grenades hanging from his chest. He had installed a machine-gun on his sidecar, manned by Sal. Together they had managed to take over the elementary school and one of the avenues leading to the bus terminal. Sal shouted something nobody understood and burst into laughter, raising his thumb. Everybody was intoxicated by combat.

3

AT THE CORNER of the street, near a two-story post office, a small group of rebels suddenly ran toward them, waving frantically. Lorenzo wondered what this was all about, until a bullet whistled by his ear, clarifying the situation. They took cover behind a burnt and twisted car wreck.

"We really tried to get them out, but we haven't managed yet," a young sergeant apologized. The name on the uniform read Samuel Hernandez. "What's more, they have hostages…"

Lorenzo scratched his head skeptically. "Hostages? In the middle of combat? Who gives a fuck?"

The Sergeant bowed his head, embarrassed. "They're friends of yours, jefe…"

"Who?"

"Two Frenchmen, I believe…"

A couple of gunshots rang from the building and they fired back at random. The exchange lasted a few seconds, then a megaphone began to scratch and spit.

"Hold your fire! We have hostages!"

Lorenzo raised his head and cupped his hands in front of his mouth. "What do you want?"

"We want to leave this place unharmed! We want a helicopter with a full tank of fuel so that we can reach Mexico City!"

"And a date with my sister," commented the Sergeant, philosophically.

"You've got half an hour! After that time, we kill a hostage!" the voice added after a second of silence, as if it had forgotten something important.

"What should we do then?" Hernandez asked.

Lorenzo reloaded his guns. "I don't know. Everything is too chaotic right now. We don't even know where the Rivas brothers are. What can I say?"

The Sergeant picked out a cigarette and lit it.

A terrible explosion shook the ground. Windows blew out from every building in the street and a blanket of black smoke-filled parts of the sky. The Sergeant had dropped his cigarette.

"The fort's ammunition depot," Lorenzo muttered.

More shots were fired. This time, inside the post office.

"These bastards are executing Marco and Patricio!" Lorenzo shouted, his voice cracking in rage and panic. "Let's go!"

They ran across the street and rushed into the ruined

entrance hall. Not a sound could be heard in the half-light, apart from the distant hiccups of automatic weapons. Lorenzo felt a film of sweat covering his cheeks in spite of the coolness inside. Crouched behind a half-destroyed interior wall, the Sergeant looked worried. Lorenzo carefully walked toward the stairs, followed by two of his men. A dark silhouette suddenly appeared at the top of the steps, soon followed by another. Lorenzo hastily stepped back, raising his guns.

"What the fuck are you doing here?" a familiar voice asked. Patricio walked down the steps, shaking his head with incredulity. Marco followed close behind, laughing in silence. Lorenzo put his guns away and stepped forward to greet them. His legs were shaking with emotion.

"What happened?" Lorenzo demanded, as they all came out in the sunlight again.

Patricio shrugged. "Well, at first, we got captured like rookies, but there's no need to talk about that. Then, they sort of tied our feet and hands, but their knots were real shitty, so we had no problem getting rid of them. When the depot blew, they were so startled that we took the chance and jumped on them, stole their weapons and gave them first class stamps to hell. You wouldn't have anything to drink, by any chance? We're dying of thirst."

4

LORENZO WALKED back upstairs to search the area where his friends had been held prisoners. He wanted to see if any interesting documents had been left behind. Four bodies lay in various positions, bathing in their blood. The place was a terrible mess. Daylight shone through the hundreds of bullet-holes perforating the walls. Lorenzo searched the cadavers, but he found nothing interesting. They were ordinary soldiers from the regular army. He had just finished frisking the last corpse, an overweight corporal with a three-day stubble, when he noticed something that chilled his spine: all four bodies had "First Class" stamped on their foreheads, in large red letters.

5

Lorenzo sat at his desk, playing with his pen. A meagre sun shone bleakly on the notebook opened in front of him. An hour ago, he had slammed his door shut, telling Lena that he didn't want to be disturbed. He had never taken an article so seriously before and she thought it was quite amusing. He didn't.

Mexico…

He tried to remember his age at the time. Twenty, twenty-one maybe. About. Maybe even twenty-two. Or twenty-three. He picked up the letter from the German magazine, Die Schwarze Fane, which topped his pile of unanswered correspondence. The tone was very respectful, which made him ill at ease. He had chosen the revolutionary path in his youth precisely to put an end to conventions and heroes. This letter treated him like a hero.

"Could you send us, dear comrade, a small article relating your participation in the Rivas uprising in Mexico in 1969? We are planning to put out a special issue on this subject and as you are one of the last survivors of this adventure…"

The word "survivor" jumped at him, as it had the first time he read it. He would soon turn forty-three. What had happened to all the others who hadn't fallen during this mad story?

He sighed and put the letter down.

A few names came back, but no faces. Since Patrizia's rape and Razelli's murder, he had intentionally erased all faces from his memory, like an old music tape on which you keep re-recording new melodies. Italy, France, U. S. A., Mexico, Japan, Egypt, France again, Denmark…Geography of escape and gloom. He was still on the blacklist in the United States, Egypt and Japan. In Italy, probably not: there was a pardon clause and the Red Brigades had taken up all of the authorities' attention for a while. In Mexico, he had no idea…

There was a knock on the door.

Jonas stepped in, a sheet of paper in hand. "Mommy told me you were writing an article. I have written one too. Do you want to read it?"

"Of course. Come on, jump in my lap."

The child sat up and lay his story over the blank notebook.

My travell to Afrika.

Last year, I went on an expedixion to Afrika with my Daddy. It was verry dangerous because there were many Krokodiles. We were looking for a misterrious river, the Black River. We crossed many jungles and Daddy got sick. Fortunatly, there was a sorcerer with us who cured Daddy with some plants. Daddy made faces and he vommitted, but after that he was better. We looked for the River everywhere and we were even attacked by Lions, but we never found it. So we went home and Mommy made us some hot chocolate.

Lorenzo smiled as he put down the paper. "So, I fell sick and vomited…Where did you find all this stuff?"

Jonas climbed down from his father's knees and picked up his story. "I saw a documentary on television and the man who talked looked like you. The rest, I made up myself. Do you think I will be a good journalist?"

"An excellent one, no doubt. I'm sure they'll have nothing to teach you at journalism school."

Lena walked into the room. "Lunch is ready, O, Great Writers."

Lorenzo stood up. The pen rolled on the table, next to the virgin notebook. "I'm coming" he said, following his son. He caressed his stomach at the sight of the food on the table. Nothing got in the way of a good meal, not even a revolution in Mexico.

6

EVENING WAS FALLING on this third day of fighting. Marco and Patricio played cards, crouching in the Opera Hall where the brigade had chosen to make its headquarters. A brasero shed a dim light on the exhausted bodies lying all around, resting under the dark chandeliers. Lorenzo lay back on the large stairs, hands crossed behind his neck. He was waiting for Sven to return from a recon mission. The Dane had left few hours earlier. There had been rumours that more American helicopters had been sighted. Marco won a hand of cards and Patricio complained loudly about his own bad luck. They had found cardboard wings in the Opera's prop closet and attached them to their backs. "Los Angeles de la Muerte," they explained, happy with their new image. From here, Lorenzo thought, they looked more like the "Clowns of Death". But, then again, in this revolution, the two were not necessarily incompatible.

After midnight Sven came back and sat next to Lorenzo. The brasero was almost out now. A faint reddish glow played on the walls and the tarnished crystals. Marco and Patricio were asleep, as were most of the men. "This time I think I've found it!" Sven whispered, his eyes shining with excitement.

"What are you talking about?" Lorenzo asked, emerging from his half-sleep.

"I'm talking about my book, of course! What a dumb thing to ask!"

"Oh yeah? And how did you find it?"

Sven brushed off the dust from his pants. "Completely by chance. I went to the fort to contact the Rivas brothers, like you told me, but one of the main streets had fallen back into the hands of the regulars, and I—"

"What street?" Lorenzo interrupted, suddenly worried.

"The Avenida Cortès, but we kicked them out, don't worry. So, like I was telling you, I had to find another way and there, in a small side street, what do I see? A bookstore, with its window still intact! A miracle, in a word. Intrigued, I took a closer look and realized it specialized in the occult...Imagine that! I wrote the address down and I'll pay it a visit as soon as I can..."

"So, what about your book?"

Sven lay down on the cold steps, using his jacket as a cover. "I haven't seen it yet, but it must be there, I'm sure of it!"

Lorenzo sighed and pulled his jacket tightly beneath his chin. It had been a long day and he didn't need another mystery to occupy his dreams.

7

EXCERPT FROM AN INTERVIEW given by Ricardo Rivas to CBS News journalist and aired on April 13th, 1969.

JOURNALIST: Why, if I may ask you this question, have you decided to engage in revolutionary action?

RICARDO RIVAS: We didn't have a choice anymore. We had been fighting through the pseudo-democratic channels to denounce the injustices created by the ruling classes for years now, without any success. The last decrees authorizing the mass expropriations in the Sonora region were the final straw.

THE JOURNALIST: Yes, but why launch such a large-scale military action without any formal warning, like a press-conference, for instance?

RICARDO RIVAS: For the shock effect. An advertised revolution is a lost revolution. Everything is already written, whether it succeeds or not. We believe in surprise. We have started the revolution, now it is up to the indigenous minorities and the poor to carry on. We are the fuse. They are the powder.

THE JOURNALIST: So, you really believe violence is the only means to attain your objective?

RICARDO RIVAS: We indeed believe that this is the only way to give a voice to the oppressed, to all those we are fighting for and with... At least, we are being heard now. Even in the

United States…You have flown down here especially for this interview, am I wrong?

THE JOURNALIST (somewhat uneasy): Our duty is to inform.

RICARDO RIVAS: That's exactly what I'm saying…(He laughs.)

THE JOURNALIST: But still, all this violence, this destruction —is it really necessary?

RICARDO RIVAS (after a moment of reflection): In some cases, I think violence must be considered as a form of dignity. Regrettable perhaps—but necessary.

TIJUANA
APRIL 20TH

1

A MILITARY MAP was taped to the central table in the Mayor's office. Sven leaned over it, carefully following an invisible path with his finger. Ricardo Rivas smoked a cigar, blinking from the smoke. Enrique stood in front of the large windows, adjusting the curtains he had just closed. The brother with no name peeked over the young Dane's shoulder. The only sound was the tick-tack of the heavy bronze clock sitting over the fireplace.

"You think he's going to find it again?" Sal discreetly asked Lorenzo, who shrugged in doubt.

Sven sighed. "I think I saw it somewhere around here…"

Ricardo moved closer to the table and looked at the spot indicated by Sven's finger. "It's only fifteen kilometers away from the American border," he grunted, chewing on his cigar. "Very hazardous." He tapped his fingers against the butts of his pistols and wordlessly interrogated his two brothers.

"It could be a good thing to control a television station, don't you think?" the brother with no name ventured. "For the propaganda."

Enrique joined them at the table. "He is right. It would be

excellent to have a propaganda base camp in this region."

Ricardo scratched the back of his head. "We have lost a lot of men and the new recruits are not 100 percent reliable. A new expedition, even a small one, seems dangerous to me. We would be weakened here, and Mexicali is too far away to send us reinforcements quickly enough in case the bastards decide to counter-attack in the next few days."

The brothers discussed this for a while. Lorenzo, Sal and Sven carefully kept their mouths shut. They knew better than to mingle in the Rivas brothers' conversations: whoever did always ended with the three allied against him. The brothers finally agreed on launching an attack, using only the minimum number of troops. Reinforcement from Mexicali would thus have time to strengthen Tijuana. Lorenzo would be in charge of the expedition. He nodded, silent, and looked at the great hall. The evening sun filtered through the curtains like long swords of fire.

2

BACK AT HIS HOTEL, after dinner, Lorenzo found Marco and Patricio playing cards as usual in the lobby. The wings were still attached to their backs, but now they were now gray with dust. He sat next to them in a leather armchair and picked up a newspaper. A car drove by in the street. Marco began to hum a song. Lorenzo sighed. He couldn't concentrate. Everything was going too fast. They had—just—managed to bring order back in Tijuana and now he had to leave again.

It seemed to him sometimes that he was running ahead of this revolution, instead of with it. Running, always running, faster, further. He wondered for a second what kind of memories he would keep of these times, if he lived long enough to remember. The future appeared to him like a threatening fog, full of tragically conventional possibilities. He tried to focus again on the paper, and he realized it was a week old. Einstein had been right: time was a relative notion, especially during revolutions.

China suddenly appeared at the foot of the stairs and called him gently. He went to meet her. They kissed before walking up the steps together.

3

WHILE CHINA was slowly undressing, he told himself he had never made love so much in so short a time. Viva la revolucíon!

4

THE JENSENS had invited them down for dinner and now, they were watching the news together. Lorenzo sat in a deep red corduroy armchair, with Lena installed on his lap. The doctor lay on the sofa. Hanna made some coffee in the kitchen. There had been a terrible earthquake in the Sonora region of Mexico. Images flashed by, showing collapsed buildings and first-aid teams desperately searching the ruins. Lorenzo thought his memories looked exactly like this.

5

CHINA, ACTUALLY, CAME FROM INDOCHINA. Her parents had sold her to a Chinese pimp who immediately sent her to Los Angeles, where a Mexican hustler won her in a poker game. The hustler brought her back to Mexico and put her to work. Lorenzo was now wearing his boots, magnificent snake-skins unfortunately sprinkled with blood stains. He had blown the hustler's brains out from a little too close.

China lay her face on his chest and caressed his stomach. Lorenzo ran his fingers through her soft black hair, perfumed with incense. A small Buddha was sitting on the night-table and China observed her devotion duties very carefully. A gentle warmth overcame him. His lips grazed the young woman's forehead. She raised her head and smiled. She could spend hours watching him without saying a word. It was China's silence that had won him over. Without words, everything seemed much simpler, even a revolution. They exchanged a long kiss. Yes, even the revolution.

6

THAT NIGHT, he had a dream about Sven. The Dane was in a room surrounded by fire, two suitcases at his feet and a fat book under his arm. His face was as jovial as ever and when Lorenzo walked through the flames to meet him, the young man embraced him with all his strength. A woman stood behind him, a small bag in her hands. There was another person, but Lorenzo couldn't make out its features through the smoke.

"Well," Sven concluded "I have to get going now. Can you step back a little?"

Lorenzo obeyed.

Sven took the book and began looking for a page. He pronounced a few words in Latin, which sounded like a succession of numbers.

A whistle tore through the rumbling flames and Lorenzo jumped in his sleep. A locomotive appeared, dragging three coaches. The train stopped in front of them. Sven hurried to the first coach, followed by his two companions. It looked like some luxury train, Orient Express style, but all the coaches were plated with silver and decorated with semi-precious stones. Sven soon reappeared at a window and waved at Lorenzo. A conductor with strange eyes blew a whistle and the mysterious convoy disappeared in the darkness.

China finally managed to wake him up. "Stop screaming

like this, you're going to wake up the entire hotel!"

Lorenzo sat up in the bed and felt his forehead. It was covered with sweat. "What was I saying?" he asked the young woman when he had finally come back to his senses.

"I don't know. You were laughing at the same time, but it sounded like "Goodbye! Goodbye!"

TÏJUANA
APRÏL 21ST

1

SITTING IN HIS BED, Lorenzo opened the envelope and took out
a couple of handwritten pages. China lay next to him, smoking
a cigarette. A young Indian boy had woken them up early to
give him this letter. In the street, the morning activity was just
beginning. He concentrated to decipher the tiny black words.

*Hello to you, Lorenzo, brother of mine, the only one that never
laughed at my crazy dreams…When you read this letter, I will
already be gone. Where exactly, I do not know, but far away. Like
you might have already guessed, yes, I have found my book. It was
in that shop. I had gone back, somewhat nervous, because I wasn't
sure that my instinct was right and I knew I couldn't take any more
disappointments. I went in anyway and a man turned around.
He immediately spoke to me in Danish. Yes, you are reading right.
In Danish! He told me his name was Christian Petersen, that he
came from a small town on the west coast of Jutland and that one
should never be surprised by anything in these parts. I asked him
then if he knew what I was looking for and he answered: "a book".
I thought I was going to fall on my ass. Noticing my surprise, he
added that as we were standing in a bookstore, this was quite
logical. He stopped dusting the books and sat down behind a desk
buried in papers. "What book are you looking for?" he asked me,
as if he already knew the answer. "El libro de Esmeralda," I said,
my voice almost failing me. He nodded, smiling. "She's behind," he*

said, pulling a greasy curtain hiding another room also filled with books. "In the reserve..." I stepped in the half-light and a woman —a beautiful woman—was crouching there, sorting books out of a crate. She noticed me and asked me what I wanted. As soon as she heard my answer, she jumped to her feet and picked out a book from the shelves, a thick in-folio bound in tarnished leather. I stopped breathing. "There you go," she said. "It's my book, but you can have it too." - "Your book?" - "Yes, my name is Esmeralda and this is my book. We are all called Esmeralda in our family and our tradition has run from mother to daughter for generations. It is said that a traveller from the north will come one day to share it, after a period of chaos. Denmark is north, isn't it?" Do as I did, Lorenzo: do not try to understand. I swear to God I am not drunk or crazy. I am writing you these lines from Esmeralda's room, who is gathering her things for our journey. I would love to be able to tell you where we are going, but it is impossible. I am not even sure myself. Maybe you will meet Christian: he is not leaving with us. If he hasn't shared El Libro before me, it is because it doesn't interest him. To live eternal truths scares him. He says he'd rather read books than live them, because that way your mistakes are not fatal. Another mystery, this boy, but I do not have time to wonder. In any case, he might explain some things to you...I do not know how much he actually knows, but like Lao Tsu said: "The wise man knows he knows nothing, and the dumb man thinks he knows everything." Only future will tell if we shall meet again. Thank you for letting me share this adventure with you. Go along your road, wherever it will lead you. Man is still the greatest mystery. A last favor: explain to the others why I have deserted them. Better yet: show them this letter. They will think I am crazy and that's perfect. Insanity sometimes rhymes with tranquility. Esmeralda tells me *she is ready. Christian just entered the room and told us he wants to come along after all. When I told you this boy was a mystery... You will therefore know nothing, my poor Lorenzo, but what does it matter in the end? See you soon, in your dreams.*

Your friend, forever,

Sven.

China killed her cigarette in the glass she used as an ashtray. "Who sent the letter?" she asked, getting up.

Lorenzo carefully folded the papers with trembling fingers.

"Who sent it?" China repeated.

2

JOE EXCHANGED a glance with Lorenzo and they both shook their heads. There was nothing left. The bookstore had completely burned down. Two firemen walked out of the rubble.

"So?" Lorenzo asked.

"Nothing. We found nothing. There wasn't anybody in here. What's more, take a look at that: none of the other buildings has been touched...a miracle."

Joe nodded once more, and Lorenzo looked at the smoking ruins. Behind them, a group of onlookers commented on the scene that nobody had witnessed.

3

SVEN...SVEN what, by the way? He couldn't tell why, but the face of his companion had suddenly come back to him. The rain was pouring over the windshield wipers and the wind bent the treetops along the road. A truck passed him, spraying blinding streams of water. Only the two red spots of the monster's taillights were visible. Lorenzo cursed and turned the wipers on full speed. With such bad weather, Jonas was going to be late for school. He focused on the road and Sven's last name. He seemed to recall now he never knew it.

1

THE PROJECTORS installed on the watchtowers swept regularly through the night, illuminating one after the other the trucks parked in front of the main building. The dentist whistled between his teeth.

"Wow, they're even more numerous than that time we got lost..."

After Sven's mysterious disappearance, Lorenzo had the luck of running into the dentist who had driven the young Dane to them. He was in the town square, advertising his dentist skills through a megaphone. Lorenzo had immediately recognized him because he wore clown makeup and his white overalls were splashed with what appeared to be blood. It was actually ketchup, but the effect was striking.

Lorenzo had him arrested immediately and escorted to the Rivas brothers' headquarters. There, he had been asked if he remembered the location of the television station that Sven had mentioned. The dentist said he sure did. They brought him a map and he pointed to a spot with great precision, a few kilometers west from the one Sven had shown.

"Still close to the border" Ricardo Rivas had muttered, but this time his observation did not trigger any discussion.

124

They had offered the dentist a full pardon for the crime of having an "unconventional medical practice" if he would guide the commando group to the television station. He immediately accepted the deal and even volunteered to fix everyone's teeth for free. They all had turned down his offer.

Lorenzo brought the infrared goggles to his eyes. "Looks like there are about fifty men, maybe more. We were right to take the mortars." He ordered his men to put the light mortars in position.

"Fire at will!" the Sergeant yelled. He happened to be Samuel Hernandez. Lorenzo had remembered him from the Marco and Patricio incident and asked him if he wanted to join the commandos. Hernandez accepted because he thought the episode with the jefe's French friends was a good story and by following the jefe again, he would surely have more good stories to tell his kids.

The first mortar shell hit one of the trucks. Pieces of metal and burning cloth spread in all directions. The gasoline caught fire and travelled to the next truck, which blew up in its turn. They could feel the heat of the fire from where they were standing. The guards from the watchtowers began to blindly shoot tracers all around. More shells exploded near the main building.

"Be careful with the antenna, goddamn it!" Lorenzo yelled.

The first wave went to attack the complex, their faces hidden behind ski-masks. Lorenzo looked at his watch. He had planned five consecutive assaults of ten men each, with a two-minute interval between them.

Hidden at the bottom of a small canyon they were virtually invisible from the station. He heard the short bursts of automatic weapons and the dry explosions of the rebels' hand grenades. The second wave got ready then took off in its turn. Lorenzo and the dentist were to go with the fifth and last wave, escorting the technicians they had brought along. The third wave hurried forward, screaming at the top of their lungs. "Tierra y libertad!"

The night was prickled with stars, but they were increasingly hidden by the thick smoke rising from the trucks. The fourth wave left running. Lorenzo let his eyes follow the crouching silhouettes gradually disappearing in darkness.

One of the watchtowers collapsed in a geyser of flames. It was their turn. Lorenzo waved at the dentist, who nodded, took a red plastic nose out of his pocket, and adjusted it to his face. "If we must die," he said with a wry smile, "let's die with dignity."

2

THEY HAD ALMOST MADE IT to the torn-down exterior fence when they realized what the noise was. They had vaguely heard it while running, but it was now loud and clear in spite of the surrounding chaos. Short loud bursts ploughed the ground and they all ducked for cover.

"A chopper!" Samuel cried. "These cabrones have a chopper!"

Lorenzo asked for the rocket-launcher and put it on his shoulder. The helicopter appeared again from behind one of the watchtowers, its lights blinking like a carnival monster. Lorenzo brought the chopper to the center of his crosshairs. He pulled the trigger and watched the missile's glowing trail. A mushroom of fire blossomed in the sky with a terrifying noise, soon followed by a rain of twisted metal. One of the remaining trucks made a screeching escape, disappearing along the potholed road.

The enemy had fled. Now they could broadcast their educational programs.

3

LORENZO STEPPED into the studio, followed by his men. A few bodies lay scattered, both rebels and regulars. The three technicians went to the switchboards. Samuel took a seat in the dressing room and a female soldier began to apply makeup to him. She was having the time of her life. Samuel would be the MC for the show later on. Lorenzo took out a collection of videotapes from his bag, enough material for the whole weekend. There was classic propaganda—interviews, speeches, documentaries—but also films like Citizen Kane and Duck Soup, and even some cartoons for the children. "Calavera Channel" wasn't going to be boring, that was certain. It was even strictly forbidden, for boredom was counter-revolutionary.

4

SAMUEL HAD JUST BEGUN TO SPEAK live in front of the cameras when a soldier knocked on the glass door of the technical booth.

"Lieutenant, there is something I think you should see—"

Lorenzo got up from his chair and walked outside, where a group of his men were waiting for him. They pointed at something on the ground—it was still smoking. Lorenzo bent over to get a better view of the object glowing in the beams of their torchlights. He felt his heart shrink inside his ribs. It was a piece of metal from the helicopter, stamped with the all-too recognizable blue and white star of the U. S. Air Force.

5

LENA WAS SITTING ON his lap, stroking his hair. Lorenzo could make out their reflections in the dark window: he, with his grey hair and tired face; she, beautiful, blonde, caring. The lamp glowed over spread-out sheets of paper, everything crossed out. On the corner of the desk, the alarm clock said 11 p.m. He had been sitting here since eight o'clock and his ass was beginning to hurt.

"What's blocking you?" Lena asked again, with her soft voice. "I saw you going in circles like a caged tiger for the past few weeks. If you don't feel like writing this article, just tell them, for heaven's sake."

Lorenzo shrugged. "They're German comrades, they're young...I know this Hans Schumacher. Well, I've met him a couple of times in Copenhagen and in Hamburg. He's very nice, enthusiastic, like us, in the good old days. I owe him this piece. He wants to know."

"Yes, but if it brings back bad memories..."

Lorenzo sighed and caressed his wife's back. "I don't know if they're bad memories...I can't remember what happened, that's the problem...I can see some faces, a few names have come back to me, but...that's it. All my life, I've trained myself to forget. Seems like I finally managed..."

Lena squeezed him in her arms. "Me too, I'd like to know

130

a little more about you... It's true that I was attracted by your mysterious side. At first. But now... I don't know how to say this to you... There's Jonas... He has a right to know..."

"You think my son wants to know that his father participated in a failed uprising in Mexico, that he killed quite a few people, slept with quite a number of women and all this to end up living a cosy bourgeois life in Denmark as if nothing happened?"

Lena shrugged.

"If it's the truth, yes, I think he has the right to know."

Lorenzo massaged his forehead with both hands. "And what about you? Do you really want to know what happened in Mexico?"

"Yes, I do."

"Even if I was a fucking loser?"

Lena couldn't help smiling. "A loser? You?"

Lorenzo moved a little on his chair, embarrassed. "When you rush headfirst into this kind of adventure with naive ideals, when your best friends get killed and you come out of it with minimal damage, yes, I think you can be considered a loser."

"And that's how you consider things happened in Mexico?"

"That's how things happened in Mexico."

"What's Metsico?"

They both turned their heads at the same time. Jonas stood at the door, in his pyjamas. He looked completely awake.

Lena jumped from Lorenzo's knees and ran to her son. "It's time to sleep, young man," she told him, frowning, but gently pushing him by the shoulder.

"But what's Metsico?"

"It's a country in Central America."

"And Daddy went there?" Lena threw a distressed glance at Lorenzo who pretended not to notice.
"Yes, Daddy went there. But that was a long time ago... Come on now, up to bed..."

Lena shut the door behind them, and Lorenzo heard them walk away: Jonas's high-pitched voice asking questions and Lena's soft tone trying to answer them. He looked again at his reflection in the window.

Loser.

6

THE DENTIST brought out a stack of files from the safe box they had finally managed to crack. "Here's some more!"

Lorenzo glanced at the station's manager's desk, rapidly disappearing under piles of papers. A national television channel, my ass! All the documents had the official C. I. A. stamp on their upper left corner.

A technician rushed into the office, looking pale. "Lieutenant, this is terrible! We are not sending anything toward Mexico—it's all going north of the border! We are transmitting to most of America's southwestern states!"

7

DAWN WAS RISING and everybody was exhausted. The programs continued to broadcast throughout the night, in spite of the risks. Lorenzo had contacted the Rivas brothers, who gave him carte blanche. He decided to take advantage of this ludicrous situation no matter what. He asked every one of his men to come and explain their struggle in front of the cameras. One could always hope to reach a fraction of the exiled community on the other side of the Rio Grande—as well as even maybe some intelligent gringos.

Lorenzo took a sip of black coffee. He wondered when the Americans would react, because they were going to react, that was for sure. By taking this goddamned station, they had involuntarily pushed the fat red button which was going to annihilate the revolution.

Ricardo Rivas had been right once again: this attack had been one attack too many. The adventure was over, it was only a question of hours. They had to stay awake, to take their last stand with courage. That was the only thing they had left now. Lorenzo gulped down another mouthful of the bitter liquid. Yes, they had to stay awake at all costs: for once there was something interesting to watch on American television...

8

INTERVIEW WITH W. W. HOBARTH, owner of KBTV, given to NBC on April 28th, 1969, and aired the same evening.

ANCHORMAN: What exactly happened this weekend on your network, Mr. Hobarth?

HOBARTH: We want to express our sincere apologies to our millions of viewers in the Southwestern states, and most particularly to all those who don't speak Spanish, for the incidents that occurred this weekend. We have been the victims of a despicable and intolerable act of international piracy, which has been condemned in the strongest terms by the Federal government.

ANCHORMAN: Is it true that your network broadcasts its shows south of the border because of the cheaper labor rates?

HOBARTH: Communist propaganda.

ANCHORMAN: These "pirates" as you have called them, declared that your network has close ties to the C. I. A. and that they can prove it. They even displayed a few documents.

HOBARTH: If you start to believe anything a communist tells you…

ANCHORMAN: If this isn't true, then what about the rumours of a covert American military operation in the area?

HOBARTH: I have no information on the subject.

EPILOGUE

1

THE NOISE of the jeep came closer and then stopped a few meters away from the body of the rider lying at the feet of his horse. A door was slammed, then another. Footsteps on the sand. A shadow leaned over the body and a conversation began between a man and a woman.

"He's dead," the man said.

"How do you know?" the woman asked. "You've not even taken a close look!" She was a middle-aged indigenous woman, wearing men's fatigues and military boots.

"He's not moving. He's dead."

The woman kneeled next to the body, turned it around with difficulty and lowered her ear to his chest. "He's alive!" she exclaimed. "He's alive! Help me, for God's sake!"

The man muttered something, but obeyed the woman. A few seagulls flew over them, screaming.

"Lorenzo!" the man said with surprise, as he helped the woman lift him up. Because of the beard, he hadn't recognized his friend.
"You know him?" the woman asked.

The man nodded.

"You bet I know him! He's one of us! A compañero! I thought those pigs had killed him."

They dragged him under the shadow of a large cluster of rocks. The man opened a canteen and wetted his handkerchief.

Lorenzo's lips were dried out. You had to be careful.

"What's his name again?" the woman asked.

"Lorenzo. He's from Italy."

"Pretty boy, that's for sure…"

The man stopped squeezing the handkerchief over his friend's face for a second.

"Hey, wait a minute! If you fall for this here fellow, I let him croak on the spot. I'm not going to save somebody's life, would he be my best friend, if my fiancée is ready to jump into his arms the second that he's cured! What's more, this guy is the most incredible sweet-talker I've ever met in my life."

The woman bent over the man and took him in her arms, rubbing her cheek against his. "You're the sexiest man in the world, Sal. You know that."

grunted with satisfaction and twisted the handkerchief
ver his friend's face.

2

It was raining.

Fat drops.

Water!

Lorenzo half-opened his mouth and his tongue tentatively licked his lips.

Fresh water!

He was saved!

He tried to open his eyes, but the sky rushed into his eyelids and burned his sight.

Water was still falling anyway.

Reassured, he fainted again.

3

LORENZO APPEARED at the door of his room and saw Sal was sitting in a folding chair by the side of the swimming pool. Lorenzo's face had thinned, but his eyes were alive. He took a few hesitating steps toward Sal who had stood up and dragged over a second chair. There were the only people around the swimming pool. Lorenzo sat down and looked around him. They were at some cheap, run-down motel, with bungalows badly in need of a paint job.

"For Christ's sakes, Sal, where are we? Heaven?"

"At the most, this is Purgatory. The owner is an old friend of mine, a retired card-player, if you know what I mean. He closed down his motel for the season. We're safe here. For a little while, at least." Sal hit the newspaper he was reading with the back of his hand. "Things are getting hot in Bolivia again."

Lorenzo looked at him. "You wanna go down there?"

Sal shrugged.

"Maybe. They might need an old guy like me, in their two-cent revolution. An excellent card-player can always prove useful." They laughed, then Sal shook his head. "Yeah, I'd like to go. But I'll have to talk to Dolly first. Actually, her real name is Dolores, but I like Dolly better. It's more chic, don't you think? In any case, she's one hell of a woman, let me tell you! Do you know how we met? We were both cheating at a poker game in some joint, in Tijuana, the one with the plastic flowers everywhere, remember? I was winning, then she was winning, we couldn't make it out. In the end we stopped, because neither of us had earned any money since the beginning of the game. We looked at each other and began to laugh and laugh! We finally ended up rolling together in some hotel bed."

Lorenzo smiled, concentrating on the shiny reflections playing on the surface of the water.

"What about you? Wouldn't you like to come with us?"

Lorenzo shook his head. "No, this adventure is over for me now. It was beautiful while it lasted, but it's over."

Sal folded his paper. "Are you sure?"

"Yes. Mexico was good, but I've got to go further."

Sal picked his nose. "Bolivia is further."

Lorenzo shrugged. "Yeah, but it's not far enough for me. I have to go somewhere that doesn't look anything like here. I've always lived that way."

Sal nodded. "Can you tell me why?"

Lorenzo sighed, avoiding his friend's eyes. "No, I can't tell you why. They say that if sharks stop swimming, they die. I'm like that too. Never drink twice from the same fountain. Why?

I don't know. Maybe because I like it like that, that's all." He looked at the sky. A fat white cloud passed by, pushed by the wind. "Yeah, I guess I must like it like that" he added, talking to himself.

They spent the rest of the day talking and contemplating the saturated blue of the swimming pool, Lorenzo trying to gather the torn pages of his memory, Sal waiting for Dolores to return from the supermarket.

That night, they ate with particular joy.

4

"Here, read this…"

Lorenzo raised his nose from his stamp collection. Bulgarian comrades had asked him to sell a few in order to set up a new trade union. "What is it?"

"It's a story your genius son has given to his teacher. Thank God, she still believes Jonas only has a wild imagination."

Lorenzo grabbed the paper and began to decipher his son's irregular handwriting.

The storie of my Daddy.

When he was young my Daddy lived in Metsico, which is a country in Central Amerika. There, he made a revoluxion with his friends and killed a lot of bad guys. He also met a lot of girls who were all in love with him, but he was in love with Mommy, so too bad for them. It was very hot in Metsico and that is why my Daddy' skinn is darker than Mommy's. Mommy also told me that a revoluxion it's a fight for justiss, so my Daddy fought for justiss in Metsico and that's why my Daddy is a hero.

Lena was still staring at him when he raised his eyes from the sheet of paper.

"It's true that he has a good imagination" he said, faintly.

Lena shook her head and snatched the story back. She slammed the door as she left the room.

Outside the eastern wind was blowing with all its strength despite the fact that they had promised spring weather last night on television. He nodded to himself and tried to concentrate on his stamps again. The promises of the weather reports were exactly like the promises of revolutions: it was always the exact opposite that happened.

5

AT NIGHT, his face turned toward the dark wall of his motel room, Lorenzo tried to recapitulate the news Sal had given him over dinner about the events that had followed the American intervention and the counterattack of the regular forces.

The Rivas brothers: on the run. There were rumours they had been arrested in Texas.

Ira, Marco, Patricio: killed in action during the fall of Tijuana. Isabela, Ira's girlfriend, had killed herself instead of surrendering. The kid had died a hero.

Manuel, Joe, the dentist: captured. Nobody knew where they were detained, or if they were still alive.

And all the volunteers who that joined them, the only ones who really had something to lose in all this? Executed, tortured, jailed. The dirty routine of lost wars.

He rolled over on his side. He could see the borderless night through the open window. All those names, getting smaller and smaller, like distant stars.

A long list, fragments of a revolution.

Tomorrow, he would say farewell to Sal and his woman, say farewell to Mexico and all his memories.